# Victor and the Fix-it Challenge

Emily Grace Ortega

*illustrated by*

Meg Ross Whalen

Copyright © 2016 by Emily Grace Ortega.
Published by Santa Fe Catholic Books.
ISBN-13: 978-1539106302

ISBN-10: 1539106306

First written edition 2016.
https://www.createspace.com/6604243

To Max, who will soon be capable of fixing anything at all, no exceptions.
-ego


To my Godsons, Brian and Sam.
-mrw

# Contents

# Trouble with Tools

## CHAPTER ONE

"Mama," Victor began as he came into the kitchen, "do you think I could spray paint the garbage can red? Because red is so much more interesting than that dark green color."

Mama turned away from the sink of dirty dishes a bit to look at him and answered, "No, Victor. I don't think that would really improve it."

"But we already have red spray paint, so we wouldn't even have to buy any."

"No, Victor." She turned back to the dirty dishes. Victor wandered off.

Quickly, Mama realized what she had just said. "Heavens!" she exclaimed, shook the dirty dishwater from her hands, grabbed a hand towel off the oven, and dashed toward the garage.

Victor looked up from his spot between the garbage can and Parsley, the dog. Victor was scrubbing at the great red streak on the side of the dark green can.

"It doesn't seem to come off, Mama," Victor said, gesturing toward the can. "But don't worry. I can still paint the whole thing red. Plenty of red paint left."

"Oh, Victor," Mama said, shaking her head sadly. "It's OK. Just leave it. But don't paint it anymore. I still don't want it to be red."

They both heard Paul start crying in the kitchen. Paul was the baby. He had just turned one. Victor thought that he was pretty cute, but he would never let Victor pick him up. He always went to Bernadette, the oldest, when he was hurt or wanted to be picked up and Mama and Daddy weren't around. It wasn't fair, Bernadette getting Paul's love like that. Also, Paul bit. He had bitten Victor and left teeth marks on his arm more than once.

"Oh, dear," Mama said, "I left Paul in the playpen. I need to go get him and finish the lunch dishes and start dinner. Please come out of the garage, Victor, and find something to do that doesn't involve spray paint." Mama hurried back to the kitchen.

Victor lingered around the garage for a moment. He spotted a screwdriver and grabbed it. He felt pretty confident that he could find something interesting to do with a screwdriver. As he went back into the house, he whistled for Parsley. "Here, Parsley!" he called. Parsley trotted into the house, and Victor patted her head. "Good Parsley! Good girl!"

Parsley was kind of a funny name for a dog, Victor thought. He spotted Bernadette sitting on the couch in the play room. "Hey, Bernadette," he called at her. "Why is Parsley called Parsley?"

"Dunno," Bernadette answered without looking up from her book.

"What're you reading?" Victor asked.

"Book," Bernadette said, still not looking up.

"OBVIOUSLY!" Victor said, and wandered on. He certainly wouldn't find anything fun to do with Bernadette when she wasn't even going to look up from her book. He looked out the big window to the backyard. Old snow covered the ground. The swing set looked cold and lonely. Even the patches of sunshine looked cold. Victor stepped into the kitchen. He glanced past it into the living room and saw Matthew and Paul playing with blocks on the floor. Matthew built a tower and Paul knocked it down. They both laughed and repeated it: build, destroy, laugh. Victor shook his head. How could they do that over and over?

He looked out at the thermometer that was fastened just outside the glass of the door leading to the backyard.

27°F

Cold. Too cold to swing. Too cold to ride bikes. Too cold for any outdoor fun, thought Victor. Too bad I don't have a solar panel on the playhouse. Then I could hook it up to a heater and play in there. Of course, I'd need to put in windows because right now the windows are just holes in the walls. All of the heat would go right out. I wonder how big of a solar panel I'd need to make enough power to heat up the playhouse. Also I'd need a door for it. There's an old piece of wood in the garage that used to be a door. I think it's about the right size for the playhouse. I just need a doorknob for it.

He began the short journey to his room, where he could sit on his bed and think about this interesting problem of upgrading the playhouse to a better, warmer, more inviting playhouse. As he walked down the hall, he noticed the door to the room Bernadette shared with Natalie was closed. There was a doorknob that didn't really seem to be doing anything. He looked at the screwdriver in his hand. Phillips. He took a closer look at the screws on the girls' doorknob. Phillips. Why not?

Victor deftly began unscrewing the Phillips-head screws surrounding the doorknob. With all his experience with a screwdriver, Victor finished in no time. He pulled out all four screws and then the knob itself. He realized that the other half of the knob was still on the other side of the door—the side of the door in the room—and now he couldn't open the door because the knob was off. No problem. He'd come back for it. He took the knob and the screws and headed for the garage to find that old piece of wood. Surely it couldn't need too much work to be turned into a door once again.

He'd already forgotten that Mama had asked him to stay out of the garage only a few minutes ago.

After examining the old door for a while, Victor grabbed a tape measure and sized up the door. For sure it was way too tall for the playhouse. But Daddy could probably help him cut it down to size with the table saw. Pocketing the tape measure, Victor headed through the door to the backyard. It took some time to get some good measurements on the playhouse doorway. For one thing, it's not easy to measure something without someone to help out. For another thing, there were a lot of rather interesting rocks between the garage and the playhouse. Victor stopped to look at a few and put one particularly greenish one in his pocket. Another rock was a dull brown color but looked like a fossil at first. It appeared to have an imprint of fish scales, but closer inspection showed that was really only some strange rocky bumpiness with dirt on it.

Once Victor finally had good measurements for both the height and the width of the doorway, he headed back toward the garage. Then he realized that he couldn't remember the width measurement. So, he walked back to the playhouse and measured it again. Then he turned for the garage again to compare the size of the door he needed with the size of the door he had. In the garage, he was surprised to find Bernadette.

"Where have you been?" she shouted at him. "Natalie's locked in our room and Mama can't open the door! She sent me to find you. Come ON!" Bernadette, who was eleven years old and starting to be a bit bossier than Victor would have liked his older sister to be, took off running for the bedroom. Victor ran behind her, excited at the challenge of getting a stuck door open.

Even from a long ways away from the bedroom, they could hear three-year-old Natalie screaming like a banshee. As they got a bit closer to the epicenter of the trouble, they could hear Mama's calm voice reassuring the little girl, "It's all right, Natalie. We'll get you out—" Then Mama's voice was drowned out by screams and sobs. "We'll get the door open," Mama called out above the noise. "Just calm down. Is Sandy your baby doll there? With her baby doll bathtub? Maybe you could give her a bath while you're waiting."

"I can absolutely NOT give her a bath while I'm waiting!" cried Natalie. "It is too alone in here. And I need the potty."

Bernadette rushed up, "I found Victor in the garage!" she announced triumphantly. "Maybe he can help."

Victor slid in to get a view of the problem door. *Uh-oh ... no doorknob.*

Mama looked over at Victor. "Do you know where the knob is Victor? We need to hurry—she's going to wet her pants."

"I didn't know she was in there, Mama. I'll go get it."

Victor ran to the garage, grabbed the missing knob, rushed back to the bedroom door, and quickly fit the knob into place. Without putting any screws in, he carefully twisted the knob and opened the door. Natalie burst out. Mama grabbed her and rushed her to the bathroom.

Victor slid down to the floor. He was in trouble again. Only half an hour after Mama had been disappointed in him for spray painting the garbage can. Mama returned after the potty business had been taken care of.

"I'm sorry, Mama," Victor offered before Mama could even say anything.

"I understand that you want to use tools and build things or change them…but you can't just take doorknobs!"

# No Tools - No Fun

## CHAPTER TWO

That evening before dinner, Victor helped set the table without arguing. It was his job this week, but he never liked to do it. After everyone was sitting at the table and Mama had dished spaghetti and meatballs onto all the plates, Mama looked at Daddy.

"Victor took the doorknob off the girls' bedroom door today, and Natalie got stuck in there.

That was after he had begun spray painting the garbage can. I'm just out of ideas. I don't know how to keep him out of trouble. I'm looking after Paul and trying to make dinner and clean up and…" Mama sighed a big sigh and repeated, "I just don't know how to keep him out of trouble."

Daddy looked at Victor, who was looking droopily at his meatballs. Victor didn't like meatballs, but he knew he was already in trouble, so he didn't mention it. Daddy looked at Mama, who was looking droopily at Victor. Daddy turned to Natalie.

"It's true!" Natalie chimed in. "I was super trapped. And I had to do potty. And Victor locked me in. And I was super trapped. And I was scared. And I had to do potty. But I couldn't because I was super trapped."

Everyone smiled a little bit at Natalie's rendering of the afternoon's events, even Mama and Victor.

"But I didn't mean to do it," Victor began. "I just needed a doorknob to fix up the playhouse a little…and I didn't know Natalie was in there. I was going to put it back."

"What about the garbage can?" Daddy asked.

"Oh," Victor said. "Well, I don't know."

"Victor," Daddy began. "This isn't the first time you've caused trouble like this. I understand why Mama's so frustrated. I think we'll just have to put the tools and paint and everything like that away. And you're not allowed to use them without express permission and supervision, which Mama and I won't be able to provide as often as you'd like. Understand?"

"Yes, Daddy," Victor said. "I understand."

"I think that's a good idea," chimed in Bernadette, "Because once Victor got the hammer and started—"

"That's enough, Bernadette," said Daddy firmly. "Victor has his consequence for causing trouble. It's not time to pick on him."

Bernadette wrinkled up her nose at Victor. He stuck his tongue out at her. "Mama!" Bernadette complained, "Did you see that?"

"That's enough, both of you!" Daddy exclaimed. "What happened that was good today?"

Mama smiled and began telling about the new words that Paul was learning to say. Victor looked droopily back at his plate of meatballs. Why did it have to be meatballs? No good dinner…No tools…No good.

\*        \*        \*


The next morning, Victor found his seat in Sister Miguel Pro's third grade classroom at St. Cletus Academy. He was right on time. Paul had been crying early that morning, so Mama was awake taking care of him, which helped her get everybody in the car in plenty of time to not be late for school. Sometimes, Mama was a little slow getting out of bed and making lunches in the morning. Other times, Paul made them late by having a messy diaper just as Mama was about to buckle him into his car seat. Then, Mama would go change him before anybody could go to school. And still other times, they were late because Natalie would take off all of her clothes after Mama had helped her put them all on. Mama would have to put them all back on her before anybody could go to school. None of those things had happened today, though, so Bernadette was sitting at her desk in the fifth grade classroom; Matthew was sitting on the circle carpet in the kindergarten; Mama was on her way back home with Natalie and Paul in their car seats, and Victor was seated at his desk.

He took a pencil out of his pencil box and went halfheartedly to sharpen it.

"Hi!" called his friend Luke, "How's it going?"

"Hi," said Victor sadly. "It's going OK. I got in trouble yesterday, and now I'm not allowed to use any tools."

"Tools?" asked Luke. "What do you mean? What do you do with tools?"

"I dunno. What do you do without tools? I mean, I can't do anything without tools. Want to build a tree house? I need a hammer, and maybe a power drill, but I was never allowed to use a power drill anyway. Want to learn how a doorknob works? I need a screwdriver. Want to adjust the hand brakes on your bike? I need a screwdriver. Want to fix the bookshelf so the shelves stop falling off those funny little pegs? I need a hammer. Want to optimize the performance of a remote control car? I need a screwdriver, maybe some batteries and wire. There's pretty much nothing to do without tools. I mean, I'll get home today and not be able to do anything at all."

"Huh. I wonder if we have batteries and wire at my house," said Luke.

Victor shook his head in disbelief and was about to ask Luke what he did for fun if he didn't use batteries and wire, but the bell rang. Sister looked at the boys. Luke went back to his seat. Victor finished sharpening his pencil and did the same.

Victor drooped through the day at school. The only good part was when Sister Miguel Pro didn't notice the pictures of airplanes he was drawing when he was supposed to be doing math. Instead, he heard her remind Susie not to draw hearts on her math paper. So, Victor quickly switched back to math and finished his page of adding before the airplanes and jet engine diagrams got him in trouble. It was easy, just adding long numbers stacked on top of each other. Sometimes math was even kind of fun, but not today. Nothing was fun with the dreary prospect of nothing to do all afternoon at home.

At the end of math, Sister went up to the chalkboard at the front of the room and wrote "Lent" in big letters. She turned back to face the class of nineteen fourth graders and smiled. "Lent," she said out loud. "Who recalls Lent from last year?"

Inwardly, Victor groaned. He recalled Lent from last year. Lent was boring. Lent was long. Lent was boring, long rosary decades prayed before bed. Lent meant that all of the statues in church were covered up with purple bags and there was nothing interesting to look at during the whole, long Mass. But he did not raise his hand and say this to Sister. Boring and long and boring, long rosaries were not the description of Lent that she was looking for.

Evangeline raised her hand knowingly. Evangeline raised her hand a lot. Evangeline did everything knowingly. Victor supposed that, with a name like "Evangeline," she had no choice in the matter.

"Yes, Evangeline," Sister Miguel Pro said, giving her permission to answer.

"Well," said Evangeline, "Lent is the forty days that lead up to Easter. It is a time of suffering and penance."

"That's true," said Sister. "Suffering and penance are important parts of Lent. However, I like to focus on renewing my prayer life during Lent. It is such a special time that Jesus gives us to draw closer to Him and recall how greatly He suffered for us on Good Friday. But it is also the time to realize again how much He offers us at Easter. It is a time to make small sacrifices that we can ask Jesus to bundle up into part of His great sacrifice, His death on the cross.

"We will observe Lent as a school by going to Mass tomorrow for Ash Wednesday. Each Friday in Lent, the whole school will gather in the church to pray the Stations of the Cross and recall fourteen moments during Jesus' suffering, crucifixion, and death. We will also have the opportunity to receive the Sacrament of Penance during school time.

"We will observe Lent as a class by reading a small section of the Gospel after our morning prayers each day. This will give us an opportunity to listen to the Word of God more frequently and keep the words and actions of Jesus more present in our minds. We will also do some special projects in religion, art, and music classes throughout Lent that incorporate the season.

"I encourage each of you to do something at home to observe Lent individually. You could make the sacrifice of giving up something you enjoy but don't need. You could commit to helping your parents or family in a specific way. Or maybe your family has a Lenten custom that you'll observe all together.

"Who would like to share a way that you'll observe Lent either as an individual or as a family? Luke?"

"Well, I'm going to try and give up video games," he said.

"That could be a very big sacrifice," Sister answered. "And what will you do during the time you generally would have been playing video games?"

"Uh…pray, I guess."

Some of the kids in the class giggled. Sister Miguel Pro smiled. "You don't have to pray all afternoon!" she said. "Maybe you could play something with your little sister? Or find your Mom and ask her if she needs help with anything. Just think of a way to be generous with your time. And of course you can pray, too. But I imagine you'd just get tired of praying if you turned ALL of your video game time into prayer time!"

Some other kids raised their hands, and Sister called on Clem.

"I'm not going to complain when Mom or Dad asks me to do my chores at home," he offered.

"That's a good one!" she said. "I'm sure that would be good for me, too—only my Mom and Dad don't ask me to do chores anymore. It's Mother Monica Anne and Sister Teresa Jerome, our principal!"

The conversation continued. Someone was giving up a TV show. Someone else was giving up TV altogether. Someone was giving up candy. Another kid was going to keep her room clean, including making the bed. Everybody was happy thinking of ways they could observe Lent. But not Victor. It had already been decided for him. He would give up tools. That would be challenging enough. He was not going to try and give up anything else, too. Well, maybe he would give up complaining about that Lenten family rosary before bedtime.

# Stuck Again

## CHAPTER THREE

Victor was sitting on the couch after school on
Ash Wednesday, not really reading the book in his lap.
Mama had finally insisted that he stop wandering
around complaining about everything in general and sit
down and do his fifteen minutes of reading for his
reading log already.

"You're making everyone sad!" she concluded.
Then, she sat him down on the living room couch and
handed him a book. He'd already read the first
chapter—something about a dog—but he was not too

interested in reading further. It had no diagrams or schematics or blueprints. Not Victor's idea of an interesting book. Just words and words and more words.

As he was wondering how many words fit on each page of this book about a dog, Mama called him. "Victor!" he heard her shout from the direction of the bedrooms. "Victor! Can you come help, please?"

Victor dropped the book and started off in that direction. He wasn't always speedy to go help Mama, but whatever it was had to be more interesting than the dog story. He quickly found Mama kneeling outside the bathroom door with Paul in her arms. She was speaking calmly to the door. From the other side of the door, he heard Natalie begin to cry loudly.

"Oh, Victor," Mama said with a sigh, "Thank heaven. Natalie's stuck in the bathroom. She's not locked in. She's stuck. The knob is stuck. I can't figure it out."

Natalie's loud sobs continued. Paul heard them and began to cry, too. Victor tried the knob. Sure enough—stuck. He peered at it closely. "I might be able to get it," he said loudly so that Mama could hear him over the two screaming children. "I need a screwdriver, though. And I gave up tools for Lent."

Mama sighed with relief and smiled gently at her sad, tool-less boy. "You gave up tools? Well, we said no tools. But this will be helpful, so it will be in keeping with Lent. I'll get you a screwdriver. What kind?"

Victor peered at the knob to make sure. "Phillips," he said.

"OK. I'll be right back with it. You stay here and tell Natalie you'll get her out."

Four and a half minutes later, Victor opened the bathroom door and released a teary-eyed Natalie.

"Thank you, Victor," she sniffled to him. "I might have been trapped in there forever, and you'd have to slide food under the door for me, and I'd grow up living in the bathroom."

"Well, I'm pretty sure that Daddy would have chopped through the door with a hatchet before he made you live in the bathroom, but you're welcome," said Victor with a smile. "Now go tell Mama that you're free."

*   *   *

When Daddy got home from work that evening, Natalie ran up to him. "Guess what?" she shouted. "Victor is not supposed to have tools. AND he gave up tools for Lent. But I was trapped in the bathroom. So Victor used a TOOL to get me out!"

"It's true," added Bernadette. "Mama said it would be in the spirit of Lent for him to free Natalie. I don't know how he does that! I couldn't figure out how to get that door open, and neither could Mama. Victor's just really good with tools."

"Well, Victor," said Daddy. "That's great to hear. I'm glad you're turning your skills away from trouble and toward good. Why don't you tell me how you managed it?"

Daddy sat down on the living room couch with Victor next to him. Matthew and Natalie snuggled up to him from the other side.

Victor told of how he had saved the day. How his experience with doorknobs had been helpful. How he stayed calm even with Natalie and Paul crying loudly and Bernadette peering over his shoulder. "I guess it's Natalie's week for being trapped," he said. "But at least this time she didn't need to worry about getting to the potty!"

Everybody laughed. It was so much nicer to have the whole family pleased with him and proud of him than disappointed in him. Mama peeked in from the kitchen when she heard the laughter. She smiled at them all on the couch together and called them to come sit at the table for dinner.

"Victor," began Daddy as he stood up. "I'll make you a deal. I'm really proud you could get that doorknob off and help Mama free Natalie from the bathroom. And I'm proud that you decided to give up your tools for Lent, especially since they've been

getting you into trouble lately. So here's the deal: Each time you fix something for us—and not something that *you* break—I'll give you a new tool. That way, you can grow your own set of tools by helping out. You'll be able to remember to use your tools to be helpful and not to cause trouble. What do you think?"

"I think that's a great deal!" Victor exclaimed. "I bet I'll have enough of my own tools to start a great project by the end of Lent!"

\*      \*      \*

That Saturday, Daddy took Victor to the hardware store. In the hardware aisle, they looked carefully over doorknobs. That bathroom that had trapped Natalie could not last another day without one. The old doorknob could not be trusted not to trap people inside the bathroom, so Daddy had simply removed it. Now, though, the door could no longer latch shut. This led to a significant lack of privacy that had caused a lot of shrieking from Bernadette as various little people wandered into the bathroom when she was already there. Those first few days of Lent had certainly been full of suffering for her. Victor didn't really mind so much. Mama, however, declared that she was tired of all the shrieking and she would not permit another day to go by without a new doorknob. So, Daddy and Victor ended up in the hardware aisle.

"Try to find one that's the same color as the old doorknob was," Daddy advised. "That way it will match the rest of the doorknobs in our house."

"Are the rest all the same color?" Victor had never noticed that before.

"Sure they are," replied Daddy. "Picture them in your mind. Not too shiny…not quite gold… not quite silver… Imagine going into your bedroom. Into my bedroom. Into the girls' bedroom. All the same shade of not quite a regular color. They're also all the same shape."

"I guess you're right. Here's the right shape!" Victor called, picking up a not quite round doorknob. "Flat on the front, right, Daddy?"

"That's it. Now do they have that one in our not quite a color?"

"Here! Right color, right shape!" Victor had another doorknob in hand.

"Sure enough," Daddy agreed after looking at it. "Although, if we're buying a doorknob for the bathroom, let's pick one that Natalie and Paul won't be able to accidently lock themselves in with."

"What do you mean?" asked Victor.

"Look," said Daddy. "If it's locked, this one needs a key from the outside to open." Daddy scanned the other doorknobs near the one Victor had picked out. "Here! Look at the outer knob on this one."

"How about that," remarked Victor. "Even if it's locked, you don't need a key. You can just use a flathead screwdriver to open it. Nobody can be locked in. I like that."

"So do I," said Daddy. "And I think Mama will find that she likes it too. Because I have no doubt that Natalie will accidently lock herself in before long. You never did it. Bernadette never did it, and neither did

Matthew. But Natalie seems to find ways to get stuck in rooms. Mama doesn't even need a screwdriver to open it really. You could do it with just the flat side of a coin. That is what I call handy. It was probably devised by a Dad with a little girl just like Natalie.

"Follow me," he continued. "We need just one more item."

Victor followed Daddy to the aisle with tools.

"How about this one? Your little reward for using a Phillips screwdriver for good and not evil," Daddy said as he picked up a Phillips screwdriver with a black and yellow handle.

Victor reached out to hold it. He felt the size of it in his palm. He pretended to unscrew something with it. He looked at the other screwdrivers on display. He reached out and picked up one with a red handle. "How about this one instead?"

"All right," Daddy agreed. "That one it is."

Together, they went to pay for the doorknob and the screwdriver. They went out to the car and climbed in. After driving for a few minutes in silence,

Victor spoke up. "Daddy," he began. "Would you keep this screwdriver for me until Easter? I mean, I gave up tools for Lent. And it is such a very nice screwdriver. I'd really want to unscrew things with it if I had it. So, maybe you could put it away somewhere safe? Then, when it's Easter you could give it to me."

"Victor, I think that is a wonderful idea. I'm very proud of you for asking. But, I think maybe you could keep it just for today. Because I know of a doorknob that needs to be installed. Think you're up for that?"

"You bet!" Victor replied enthusiastically. "I can get that doorknob in. No trouble at all!"

"Great! After that job is complete, I'll be happy to take custody of your Phillips screwdriver until Easter."

# The Leaky Faucet

## CHAPTER FOUR

After Mass on that first Sunday of Lent, Victor
and Matthew went out to play in the backyard. It was
nice and sunny. The air had frost in it, but the only
snow around was in the shadows. After Victor and
Matthew chased each other for a while, Natalie joined
them. She was bundled up head to toe, and the boys
laughed when they saw just her little green eyes

peering out between a lavender stocking hat and a green scarf.

"Hi, Natalie!" Victor called. "Want to play tag?"

Neither boy could hear her answer from under that scarf, so Matthew started chasing her. Victor chased Matthew. Parsley the dog showed up and chased Victor. The chain of children followed by the dog raced around the back corner of the house. Natalie slid on an icy spot that she didn't see. Thump! She crashed to the ground with a scream. Matthew couldn't stop in time, slammed into her, and landed right on top of her with a yelp of his own. Victor stopped fast and only bumped into the pile of younger siblings. Parsley thought the whole pile-up was great fun and began to run circles around the kids, barking loudly and happily. Natalie continued to howl from the bottom of the pile.

Mama popped out through the kitchen door. "Is everyone all right?" she called, trying to see what had happened.

"We're fine, Mama!" Victor announced as he pulled Matthew off of their little sister. "Natalie just slipped on some ice."

"OK," Mama answered. "You're all right, Natalie?" Mama always wanted to make sure that everyone was all right. And then she would make sure again.

"I will be all right," Natalie sniffled from somewhere under her thick scarf. "Matthew crashed me. But Victor pulled him away. But I am not chasing anymore."

Mama smiled. "Go ahead and play outside a little longer. It's such a lovely, sunny afternoon for the cold of winter." She popped back through the door and was gone.

Matthew chased and tackled Parsley and lay on top of the dog. Victor, however, had lost interest in chasing. He was looking at the ice that had caused Natalie to slip. He followed it with his eyes. There was a small trail leading back to the wall of the house, right to a water spigot. The spigot was dripping!

37

"Hey, Matthew!" Victor called. "Look at this! The faucet is dripping!"

Matthew looked up from his spot on top of the dog. Parsley took advantage of his distraction to leap out from under him and bound away. Matthew wandered over and looked at the drippy faucet with his older brother. Natalie approached cautiously.

"I think you should fix that, Victor," she commanded more than suggested. "Because then that slippy ice won't slip me down any more."

"That's a good idea, Nattie," Victor replied. "Let me see…"

Victor peered at the handle on the faucet. He wiggled it. It still dripped. He turned it on. Water gushed out.

"Hey!" Natalie complained as her little fur-lined boots got wet. "That's my boots!"

Victor turned the water off. It dripped. He wobbled the handle and looked at it closely. "I think I've got it," he remarked to no one in particular. Matthew had already wandered off to play with

Parsley. Natalie continued to watch Victor curiously but had stepped back to keep her boots dry.

Victor went to the kitchen. "Mama," he said as he entered. "May I use a flathead screwdriver? I know it's Lent, but I think I can fix that drippy faucet in the backyard."

"Oh, dear," Mama replied as she wiped her hands on a dish towel. "Is that dripping again? I thought we got it fixed last fall."

"It is dripping," Victor confirmed. "Natalie slipped on the ice that it made. But don't worry. I think I can fix it. I need a screwdriver first."

"Well, you're welcome to try," Mama said. "You just stay here with Paul I'll be right back with that screwdriver."

"Sure," replied Victor as Mama left the room. He turned to his youngest brother who was buckled into a high chair, munching Cheerios off of his tray. "Well, Paul, looks like I'll earn another tool pretty quickly here. This isn't too hard at all. Two screwdrivers. I can do a lot with one Phillips and one flat."

Paul just looked at Victor with big, baby eyes. Victor picked up a Cheerio. Paul reached out to grab it away from him. Victor laughed. Paul laughed because Victor was laughing.

"Oh, Paul!" said Victor. "You're funny!" He grabbed a Cheerio and lobbed it at Paul's head. Paul looked surprised at first and then laughed a joyful baby laugh. The only things in Paul's world were his big brother and Cheerios bouncing off his head. And what a fun world that made! Victor kept throwing them, and Paul kept laughing. The big boy and the little boy were both laughing. Victor put a fresh handful of Cheerios on Paul's tray and continued to lob Cheerios at the baby's head. Paul laughed and clapped and squealed with delight.

Bernadette peaked her head into the kitchen to see what was so funny. "Oh. My. Goodness," she said quietly, as if those three words were three complete sentences. "Boys are SO ridiculous." She disappeared before Victor even noticed her.

Victor didn't notice Mama return either. Mama stopped short as she entered the room. "Victor Patrick West," she began in her serious voice. Victor turned suddenly. His laughing smile froze. Paul squealed one last delighted squeal and became solemn at the sudden silence and absence of Cheerios hitting him in the face. Mama looked at her biggest boy and her littlest boy. Suddenly, she laughed. "Oh, Victor!" she exclaimed. "I'll take back the Patrick West. I suppose Paul was enjoying playing with his big brother. Toss a few more at him. Here's your screwdriver. Just go get the broom and sweep up those Cheerios before you start in on any drippy faucets."

Victor smiled at Mama and started the baby laughing again with another barrage of cereal flying through the air.

\*       \*       \*

After forty minutes by himself in the cold, Victor's mittens were thoroughly wet, and he was thoroughly frustrated with the still-dripping faucet. He had tightened that screw in the middle. Still dripping. He had loosened that screw, then tightened it again. Still dripping. He had taken the handle all the way off, looked at the screw, cleaned it off on his mitten, fit the whole thing back together, and tightened it up. Still dripping. Now he sat looking at the dripping faucet with no handle. The handle, the screw, and the screwdriver lay on the slick, icy, wet ground in front of him. He was out of ideas and out of patience and out of warmth, too. It had seemed so easy to fix a drippy faucet. What had gone wrong? He continued to stare at the problem. Where *was* the problem? The handle? The screw? The faucet? Somewhere deep inside the wall of the house? Who knew where those pipes went?

If the problem was past the wall, there was nothing to be done. Mama and Daddy would never let him open up the wall. But, Victor reasoned, the drip is at the faucet, so the solution must be at the faucet. Faucet. Faucet. Faucet. What a funny word. What a funny sound. Faucet. Faucet. Fau—Wait! I've got it. That's not the only faucet. We have lots of faucets. I just need to look at a faucet that doesn't drip and figure out what the difference is. Then, I make the drippy faucet like the non-drippy faucet. Problem solved!

Victor grabbed the screwdriver and jumped up. He dashed around the corner of the house, through the gate and into the front yard. There was another outdoor water faucet popping out of the house! He examined the ground nearby. No ice. No ice meant no drip! This was a good faucet. He looked at it closely. The handle was the same. He turned it on. Water poured out. He turned it off. The water stopped. He waited a moment. No drip. Perfect.

With his screwdriver, he unscrewed the screw in the center of the handle, carefully so that the water would not come on. He held the handle and the screw in his mittened palm. They looked exactly like the ones from the drippy faucet. He frowned. Maybe this wasn't going to work after all. He looked at the front faucet again. No drip.

He took the handle and screw to the backyard. He compared them with the other handle and screw on the ground near the drippy faucet. The two handles appeared exactly the same. The two screws appeared exactly the same. Victor sighed with defeat and picked up the pieces to put the front faucet back together. Suddenly, he noticed something. When he held the two screws, both in his palm at the same time, he realized that they were not exactly the same. They were only *almost* exactly the same. The screw from the good faucet was just a bit longer. That was it! The drippy faucet needed a longer screw!

Victor dashed to the kitchen with the longer screw. He took off his mittens and opened the tool drawer. Pushing tiny nails, big nails, a tape measure, and a few picture hooks aside, he looked for a screw like the one he had removed from the faucet that did not leak. A hammer, a few safety latches that prevented babies from opening doors and cupboards, an electric outlet cover, a few tiny screws, a very large bolt with a hex nut, a pair of broken sunglasses… This drawer seemed to have a little bit of everything that Victor was not looking for. Victor spotted a screw! He matched it up to the one in his hand. It was too short. He kept looking. Another one, but it was nearly as long as his hand. He quickly recognized it as leftover from when Daddy had built the little picnic table last summer. There! A shiny brass-colored screw! It looked just right. Victor carefully laid it on the counter next to the one he needed it to match. It was a perfect fit!

Victor grabbed the pair of screws and dashed back outdoors without even putting his mittens back on. First, he used the original screw to tighten the handle onto the faucet that had not been dripping.

Then he approached the drippy faucet. He looked at it and took a deep breath. Could he do this? Was this screw really the answer that he needed to solve the problem of the drippy faucet? Wouldn't Mama be

surprised and happy if he made the dripping stop! Wouldn't Daddy be proud of him!

Carefully, he aligned the handle with the knob sticking out of the faucet. He inserted the point of the screw into the center and fit the flat tip of the screwdriver into the groove of the screw. He held his breath as he twisted. The screw was finally tightened, and the handle looked great. But it had looked great before he had started trying to fix it. He didn't need it to look great. He needed it to not drip. Slowly, Victor turned the knob clockwise and watched the water come out of the faucet. He forcefully turned the knob back counterclockwise and saw the stream of water lessen and then stop. He watched closely and saw a last drip of water. He watched for another half minute. He saw no drips. With a cautious smile decorating his face, he watched for another half minute. The smile grew and grew as he watched for a full two minutes and saw no drips.

Victor transformed his huge grin into whistling. As he whistled joyfully, he picked up the screwdriver and faulty little screw. He had conquered a problem that had bothered both his parents for months. There would be no more icy puddle forming in front of the spigot. Maybe he'd find some rock salt for that patch of ice so no one would slip on it anymore, either. And he'd give Daddy a call at work and see if maybe he had time to get a new flathead screwdriver for Victor's collection on his way home.

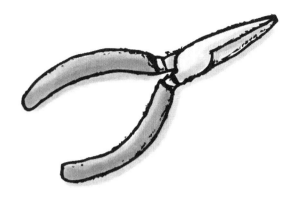

# The Power of Prayer

CHAPTER FIVE

Slowly, the snow melted away until only small, dirty patches remained in the shady spots of the yard. Still, it was cold enough that playing outside for more than a short game of tag wasn't much fun. So, Victor drooped through days at school and afternoons at home. He was forced to read dull books and write pages of dull math problems. He was forced through family rosaries and family dinners featuring soups full of icky carrots or meatloaves sprinkled throughout with little specks of onion. Lenten Fridays were a welcome relief for Victor. Mama had some tasty Friday meatless recipes that Victor looked forward to.

On this particular Friday, Victor walked into the kitchen to investigate what was starting to smell so good. Natalie was standing on a chair next to Mama patting cornmeal onto pieces of raw fish. Victor smiled. He knew that Mama would take those pieces of fish, put them in the frying pan with hot oil, and fry them until they were golden and crispy. Served up with a squeeze of fresh lemon, crispy fried fish was the best dinner possible.

"Mmm! That looks good, Mama!" Victor said happily. "Does Natalie really know how to do that? I don't want her to mess it up."

"She won't mess it up," Mama assured Victor with a smile. "This part is simple. I can't let her do the frying, though. It would be too easy for her to get burned. She's not quite tall enough to reach the stove.

Have you seen Bernadette? I need her to start setting the table for dinner."

"I'll go look for her," Victor offered. What a great evening! Crispy fried fish to look forward to, and it wasn't even his turn to set the table.

A short while later, Victor sat down for dinner with the rest of the family. After Daddy chased Parsley out from under the table, he led the family in prayer:

*Bless us, O Lord, and these Thy gifts*
*Which we are about to receive*
*From Thy bounty, through Christ Our Lord.*
*Amen.*

Mama began to dish the crispy fish, fried potatoes and steamed broccoli onto plates and pass them out.

"Where are the gifts from high county?" Natalie asked loudly. "Every time we are eating, we talk about it."

Bernadette smiled.

Victor looked puzzled. Then he understood. "Oh! I think you mean 'from Thy bounty,' not high county."

Daddy smiled and said, "Thy bounty means God's generosity. The gifts are our dinner—we need to thank God for the food He gives us."

"But Mama bought it at the grocery store," Natalie disagreed. "I'm sure she did. She made me go with her, and I could not sit in the cart because Paul is smaller, and I had to carry bags into the kitchen from the car. And it was all food. She bought a lot of food, and that's the food we eat at dinner every day. From the grocery store. Not from God."

"Wow," sighed Bernadette rolling her eyes. "Pass the lemons, please."

"Mama buys it with money I earn at work. God has given me a good job and made me healthy, so I can do my job and buy food for my family. Everything we—"

"May I be excused?" Victor interrupted. The crispy fish had been delicious, but now he was ready to get away from what seemed like a boring conversation.

"Not so fast. Let Daddy finish explaining," Mama said, denying him permission to leave.

"I get it," answered Victor. "God gives us our food, Natalie. And our clothes and our home and our dog. Everything. May I please be excused?"

Paul began banging his sippy cup on the tray of his high chair.

"How was school today, Victor?" Mama continued, louder, so she could be heard over the noise Paul was making. She had once again denied permission to leave the table.

Victor knew what that meant: he couldn't leave the table until he answered. "Fine," he replied. "Now may I be excused?"

"We had Stations of the Cross," Bernadette offered. "I don't like them. Too sad. But I like the part at the end where Father does the nice-smelling smoke."

"Incense," corrected Victor. "It's called incense, Bernadette." He gave up on asking to be excused.

Paul had switched from simply banging the tray with his cup to using the cup to smash a piece of broccoli into a piece of fish. The noise did not really decrease with the change. The mess just increased. Victor chuckled at the baby.

"I KNOW," answered Bernadette loudly. "I know it's called incense. Victor. I just said nice-smelling smoke so Matthew and Natalie would know what I was talking about."

"I know it's called incense," objected Matthew. "Do you think I don't know about incense? I'm in kindergarten!"

"We know you're in kindergarten," Bernadette said. "And of course NOW you know it's called incense because we just said it."

"I knew before…"

"May I PLEASE be excused?" Victor thought the time had come to ask again.

"I think I'll be excused," responded Daddy, standing up. "You may be, too, Victor."

"Thank you! That conversation was getting painful."

Mama looked up from wrestling the sippy cup away from the baby, who was also trying to shove something into his mouth. "Victor, please clear the table. Bernadette, please bring the rosaries into the living room. Everyone come into the living room in six minutes for Lenten Rosary."

"Why six minutes?" asked Bernadette as she stood up.

"Do we have to pray the Rosary?" added Victor. "We already prayed Stations of the Cross at school."

"If you can tell me all the Stations of the Cross—from memory—you don't have to pray the Rosary with us," offered Daddy.

"Please don't do that." Mama gave Daddy a tired look.

"May I have that deal?" Bernadette didn't wait for an answer. "Number One: Jesus is condemned to death. Number Two: Jesus—"

"The deal is for Victor only," Daddy responded. "With Mama's approval. Do you think he really knows them, Caroline? Do you even know how many there are, Victor?"

"A lot." Victor answered. "Number One: Jesus is condemned to death. Number Two: Jesus…falls. Then He falls again. Then Mary is there. Then Veronica. Then He falls again. Then He dies. Then Mary again. Then the tomb. I think that's it."

"Not a bad abbreviated version," commended Daddy. "But it looks like you'll be praying the Rosary after all, much to your mother's relief. I'll help you clear, though, in recognition of your efforts."

\*　　\*　　\*

The family re-assembled in the living room. Bernadette passed out the rosaries. She handed Paul a rosary made out of extremely fat, colored wooden beads. Mama set Paul and his fat Rosary on the carpeted floor near her feet. Bernadette sat on the couch next to Mama with her feet near Paul, too. The rest of the family arranged themselves on the other chairs.

"I believe in God, the Father almighty…" began Daddy. Then he asked Mama to lead the first sorrowful mystery, the Agony in the Garden. During the second Hail Mary, Paul started squiggling around and making noise, so Bernadette moved and sat next to him on the floor. She tried to show him his beads and draw his attention to the colors, but Paul was more interested in grabbing at Bernadette's shiny crystal rosary. Finally, he got a good hold on it. Bernadette gave it a sharp pull in the opposite direction, and— pop! It was no longer a nice long loop. The beautiful crystal beads drooped limply from Bernadette's hand to the floor in a single line.

"Paul!" cried Bernadette. "You ruined it." She sniffled to hold back the tears that were so near.

"That's the rosary Mama and Daddy gave me for my First Communion."

Mama paused the prayer. Everyone, even Paul was silent for a long moment.

"Let me see, Bernadette," Victor said, reaching his hand out. She gave him the rosary, and he only needed a glance to figure out what he needed to do. "I can fix that with needle-nose pliers. It'll be easy," he handed it back to her.

"May he do it now, please, Mama?" asked Bernadette. "So I can finish praying?"

Mama looked hesitant, glanced at Daddy's large smile, then smiled gently at Bernadette and Victor. "Yes, he may. Go ahead and find the pliers, Victor. But please bring them back here and keep praying with us as you work on it."

Victor handed Bernadette his own rosary and dashed off to locate a good set of needle-nose pliers. He was back in a flash. He sat with the family, working with the pliers and answering the prayers. Praying flew by that way. Bernadette had her rosary back in hand for the last decade. Bernadette gave Victor a thankful smile, and he beamed in return.

After the final, "Amen," Victor said with a big smile, "Bernadette, that's the only way to pray!"

# A Leaky Toilet

## CHAPTER SIX

Wednesday morning, Victor woke up with a smile on his face. He'd finished his homework. It was already tucked into his backpack. When he walked into the kitchen, Mama had his favorite cereal—shredded wheat *with* frosting—in his dish with milk in a cup next to it. He poured the milk onto the cereal, and then

61

he remembered. It was Wednesday. That meant Mass at school. Mass was long. He got in trouble with Sr. Miguel Pro if he didn't kneel down or stand up or sit down at the correct times. Sr. Miguel Pro had gotten frustrated with so many of the boys so many times during school Mass that now she made them sit in assigned seating. They had to sit boy, girl, boy, girl. So, Victor had no chance of sitting next to any of his friends. He usually sat by Stella or Miriam during Mass. They were both all right. Stella could run pretty fast, and Miriam could do at least six different bird calls that actually sounded a lot like real birds. Both of them were pretty serious about sitting quietly and nicely during Mass, though. That was OK for them, but it just made Sr. Miguel Pro notice that much more when Victor was fidgeting and not paying attention.

Mama got them to school right on time. Bernadette and Matthew bounded out of the car, calling good-byes to Mama and the little kids and blowing kisses. Victor dragged himself out. Mama called him back to get his backpack. He did and then shuffled off. Mama called him back again to get his lunchbox. He shuffled back towards the car. Paul squealed and waved frantically at Victor, who did not wave back.

"Have a great day, Victor!" Mama called happily. Victor lifted his hand in a half-hearted wave but did not turn back to call anything happily to Mama. Mama smiled to herself and drove off with Natalie and Paul, those fortunate little kids who didn't have to attend school Mass.

*       *       *

Sr. Miguel Pro jumped right into a grammar lesson after Mass. It wasn't that Victor didn't appreciate grammar. He'd actually thought about it once and decided that grammar was rather useful. Take Paul, for example. He possessed no grammar. He couldn't do anything. Well, if it came to that, he could barely walk, either. Between walking and grammar, Paul really had no power at all. Victor was very glad he had successfully acquired both those skills. It gave him a lot more power than a helpless little chubby baby sitting on the kitchen floor and banging pots with a wooden spoon. On second thought, that might be a better way to spend the morning than sitting in a school desk, banging away at grammar with a wooden pencil.

Victor dutifully added some capital letters and commas to the sentences on the grammar page on his desk. Four sentences ended with periods, two with question marks, one with an exclamation point.

"Pass your papers in," announced Sr. Miguel Pro cheerfully. "Please take out your math workbooks now."

Victor dug around in the desk for the required math book and opened up to the right page. He zipped through the multiplication problems while Sister was giving the explanation and managed to finish as everyone else was starting. He looked around and smiled. He started drawing a skyscraper on the edge of his math page and wondered how he could make a building strong enough to be that tall. It would need more than just wood. It would need something stronger. He finished the skyscraper. He looked around. The rest of the class was still hard at work multiplying. Victor raised his hand.

"May I use the restroom?" he politely inquired when he was called on. "I'm already finished with my math."

"Go ahead," Sister granted him permission with a smile.

As Victor was drying his hands and getting ready to head back to the classroom, he noticed a sound coming from the toilet. It was the sound of water running. He went back and looked at the toilet. Sure enough, water was continually flowing into the bowl. He jiggled the flushing handle and waited. That usually stopped a toilet from running. This one did not stop, though. Victor was puzzled. He carefully lifted the heavy lid off of the tank behind the toilet and set it gently on the floor. He peered into the tank. All of the pieces of the flushing mechanism looked pretty old. He started adjusting them here and there. He tugged at the chain. He lifted the flap up and down. He examined each bit, trying to discover what wasn't operating just as it ought to.

*     *     *

About fifteen minutes later, Luke walked into the bathroom. He found Victor seated on the floor of the bathroom with an assortment of toilet parts around him.

"Victor! What are you doing?! Sister sent me to come make sure you were OK since you'd been gone for so long. But you're going to be in huge trouble! You can't just take toilets apart!"

"Well, I'm not taking toilets apart. I'm taking one single toilet apart. And believe me, it needed to be done. Look at this flapper," Victor waved a thin pole, with a reddish, rubbery disk on the end of it, in the air above his

66

head. "It's ancient! No wonder the toilet was not working properly. As long as you're here, would you mind coming back with some white glue? Or tacky glue if you can find it. This really needs some new parts, but I think I can make a temporary fix with glue."

"Victor, you know I have to tell Sister Miguel Pro what you're doing, right?"

"Sure. Are you guys still on math? I was finished with math. Thought I might as well do something useful."

"Uh, OK. I'll go see about that glue, I guess." Luke walked off.

Two minutes later, Victor heard a sharp knock from the doorway followed closely by the principal's voice, "Victor West? Is anyone else in there using the facilities? I need to come in."

"Come on in, Sister. It's just me. I'm fixing this toilet up."

Sister Teresa Jerome entered the boys' room and stopped abruptly just inside the door. "Heavens!"

she said as her eyes widened. For Sister Teresa Jerome, this utterance expressed the height of shock, frustration, disbelief, surprise, and just about every other emotion. This was as close as she came to being rendered speechless.

"Victor, what do you think you are doing?"

"I'm fixing the toilet," Victor answered calmly. "Luke didn't happen to ask you to bring glue, did he?" Victor looked up at Sister.

Sister peered curiously at the assortment of bits surrounding her student. "I notice there's no water in this toilet," she ventured to say.

"No. I turned it off. Emergency and repair shut-off valve," Victor tapped a knob coming out of the wall. "Less likely to make a mess that way."

"I am glad you concerned yourself with avoiding a mess," Sister offered as she eyed the bathroom wonderingly. *If this is Victor's idea of NOT a mess...heavens!*

"Victor, I need you to accompany me to my office immediately," Sister commanded, regaining her composure as Sister Teresa Jerome, principal of St. Cletus Academy. "Well," she continued, feeling some of that composure again slip away. "Could you first please return at least one toilet to working condition?"

"Sure thing, Sister," Victor answered. "Only this one here is out of order. The others will be fine as soon as I twist the emergency shut-off valve back the other way." With a twist of the knob, Victor hopped to his feet and trotted happily after Sister. How could she fail to be delighted that he was improving her school?

\*      \*      \*

After a brief interview with Victor, Sister Teresa Jerome dispatched the nonplussed third grader back to his classroom. She smiled to herself as she turned to her computer to send an email to Victor's parents:

*Sister Teresa Jerome, principal*

**To [Mr. Martin West] [Mrs. Caroline West]**

*Dear Mr. and Mrs. West,*

*Victor will need to remain after school for twenty to thirty minutes today to assist Mr. Vasquez, our maintenance man, in re-assembling a toilet. After using the bathroom this afternoon, it seems that Victor detected an inefficiency with our commode and took it upon himself to repair it. He got as far as separating most of the parts of the toilet. At that time, Sister Miguel Pro became concerned about how long Victor had been gone and sent another student to make sure Victor had not fallen ill or met another misfortune in the boys' room. I have spoken with him about the necessity of all things in their place. Next time he discovers an imperfection in our school, he understands that he is to first seek permission before attempting a repair or gathering tools to fix it.*

*His only discipline for this highly unexpected repair session will be to remain after school and complete the repair. If it helps your family schedule,*

*Bernadette and Matthew may remain after school with the children who stay for after-care. This way, you can pick up all the little Wests at once.*

*Sincerely in Christ,*

*Sister Teresa Jerome, O.P.*

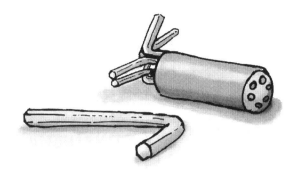

# Bedtime Fixes

## CHAPTER SEVEN

A half hour after school got out, as she climbed into the car, Bernadette declared, "Hey, Victor, after-care is kind of fun. Maybe you should get in trouble more often so we can go to after-care. I got to do this neat project with glitter."

"I wasn't in trouble," Victor objected. "I volunteered to fix the toilet in the boys' bathroom. HUGE difference. Huge. In fact, Sister Teresa Jerome said I am welcome to offer to fix anything in the school. She just recommended I let her know ahead of time and set it up with Mama so that she has more notice that I'll be staying after."

"Well, good job," said Bernadette. "I've never heard of a kid helping fix stuff around school before. And you're only in third grade. That's pretty impressive."

"I'm glad that Sister appreciated your help, Victor," Mama chimed in. "But she is correct: I would definitely appreciate a little more heads-up when you're going to stay late. It worked out nicely today, though. Paul was napping, and I was just as glad to let him sleep the extra half hour. I never like to wake up a sleeping baby."

At home that afternoon, Victor heroically did quiet reading for his school reading log. Once again, it was a book with no diagrams or blueprints. That meant it was not a favorite book of his. However, the story in it was about a kid who got lost in the woods. He learned how to make fire and catch animals to eat and basically live like a wild man. So, the story was all right. It made Victor wonder if there were any woods around his home where he could get lost and live like that. The difficulty would be that he wouldn't want to get lost right now. Too cold. Maybe sometime after Easter it would be warm enough to get lost in the woods for a week or so. Victor was sitting with the open book in his lap, looking out the window and thinking about how he could survive in the woods until someone found him, when Natalie bounded officiously into the room.

"It is time for dinner!" she announced proudly.

"OK," Victor replied without moving.

"That means you must come sit at the table," Natalie continued, her little hands on her hips. She was very determined to accomplish the task that Mama had assigned her: invite everyone to come sit down for dinner.

"I know that," answered Victor, still without moving.

"Well…I'm coming back to check on you!" she said and bounded off to find her next invitee.

Glancing around for a bookmark but not finding one, Victor shut his book, put it on the coffee table, and went to the dinner table.

The meatloaf had arrived before he did. He did not care for meatloaf. He looked around the table. Everyone else seemed delighted with meatloaf. Natalie and Matthew had not yet arrived. She's probably bossing him into coming to dinner, thought Victor as he flopped down into his chair.

Victor struggled through dinner. He re-arranged the meatloaf on his plate many times. Every time Mama asked him to please eat his dinner, he had a nibble. The sweet potatoes weren't too bad. Finally, Victor deemed that he had consumed enough of the meatloaf to qualify his dinner as having been eaten.

"May I please be excused?" he asked as he stood up.

"Yes, you may," Mama answered, glancing at his plate. "Please clear your dishes. And then come into the living room for family Rosary in a few minutes."

Victor groaned inwardly. Outwardly he slowly cleared his dishes, then looked around for something that desperately needed to be fixed. If he was fixing something important, maybe he could be late for Rosary. Nothing seemed to be broken, though, and the family was re-assembling in the living room already, so Victor joined them.

He fished his Rosary out of the basket. "I believe in God, the Father almighty..." Daddy began the prayers. Everyone else joined in, and the sorrowful mysteries were underway.

"Victor," Daddy said softly after the *O My Jesus* prayer. "Would you please lead us in the second decade?"

"The Second Sorrowful Mystery," Victor announced loudly in response to Daddy's request. "The Crowning with—

"Second is the Scourging," Mama whispered gently.

"The Scourging at the Pillar," Victor announced without stopping. "For this mystery, we remember how Jesus was tied to the pillar. His hands were tied up. He couldn't get away. Then the soldiers whipped him. Not with a regular whip. With this whip that had sharp bits of metal and glass and nails sticking out of it. Lots of them. And he started to bleed. And they kept—"

"I think that's a good enough description," Mama said softly with a glance at Natalie's wide and frightened eyes. "Let's begin the prayers now."

"Our Father…" Victor dutifully began.

The Rosary continued without anything breaking. Once the rosaries were tucked back into their basket, the kids headed off to get ready for bed. Matthew flipped on the switch in the hall. The light from the bulb swelled into a powerful glow, flickered, and left the hallway in darkness.

"Finally!" Victor exclaimed. "Something to fix! Matthew, could you bring in a chair for me to stand on while I get a new light bulb out?"

Matthew trotted off to drag in a chair while Victor went in search of a new bulb. Both boys returned, and Victor hopped up onto the miniature chair that Matthew had brought from the play room. Creak! Victor hopped back down and peered under the chair. The support dowel appeared to be loose, very loose. And cracked! Nothing a little wood glue and an Allen wrench couldn't fix.

"You find another chair, Matthew," commanded Victor. "I can fix this one with glue and an Allen wrench."

Once again, both boys returned with different repair items. Victor hopped, once again, onto the new chair. It held. He handed Matthew the new light bulb, unscrewed the old one, and then traded bulbs with Matthew. Twist, twist, twist, hop to the floor. Victor flicked the switch and there was light in the hallway.

"Thanks, boys!" called Mama happily. "Now come get ready for bed, please!"

"This chair needs to be fixed, too, Mama," Victor countered. "May I do that before bed?"

"OK," she agreed, "But Matthew, you come get ready for bed, please."

Matthew drooped off toward the bedroom while Victor tried different size Allen wrenches until he found the right sized one. A few minutes later, the glue was drying, and the chair was looking whole again. It would be ready for use in the morning.

Victor skipped toward his bedroom, but before he reached it, a sad-looking Natalie bumped into him. She held up a little brass-colored knob.

"It came right off of my dresser!" she announced, clearly somewhat happy with her small misfortune. "I cannot open my drawer now. My pajamas are trapped in there."

Victor took the knob from her and peered at it.

"I think I can fix this. I just need a screwdriver. I happen to have my own screwdriver, you know. Come on." Victor continued toward his bedroom.

"Don't fix it too fast, though," Natalie commanded as she trotted along behind him. "Because my pajamas are trapped in there. I don't mind staying up while you get it fixed."

Victor smiled to himself at his little sister's plan to stay up past bedtime. He pulled open his sock drawer and felt around for his screwdriver. Not there. He started pulling out socks and tossing them on the floor. Now he could see the bottom of the drawer, covered with old Christmas paper. He peered in. No screwdriver. He lifted the paper. No screwdriver. He felt around the drawer again. Nothing. He opened the underwear drawer and felt around under the pairs of underwear just in case he had put the screwdriver there instead. Nothing. He groaned. How could his brand new screwdriver be missing?

# Stations of the Cross

## CHAPTER EIGHT

Victor turned around, "Natalie, have you seen my screwdriver? You can tell it's mine because it has a red handle. Daddy's screwdrivers have black with yellow."

Natalie shook her head no. "I guess this means that my pajamas are still trapped. Oh well."

Victor put all the pairs of socks back into their drawer. He looked on top of his dresser. He shared the room with Matthew, so he looked on top of Matthew's dresser, too. Nothing. He picked up some dirty clothes off of the floor and tossed them into the laundry basket. He found nothing underneath them. He checked under the bunk beds. He opened the closet. He rifled through the shoes, slippers, and boots on the closet floor. Nothing. He went off to find Mama. She often knew where things were when they were missing.

He spotted her in the room that Natalie shared with Bernadette. She had pulled out the drawer above the one missing its knob. This allowed her to reach down into the drawer below and, much to Natalie's disappointment, pull out a pair of pajamas.

"Mama," said Victor. "I'm missing my new, red-handled screwdriver. Have you seen it? Once I find it, it'll be simple to fix Natalie's knob."

"I don't think I've noticed it anywhere," Mama replied. "I'm missing Paul. He needs to go to bed. Have you seen him?"

Victor turned and glanced into the hallway.

"Yes!" he pointed toward Paul. "There he is! He's walking! Really walking all by himself!" Victor laughed and began walking toward Paul. "Hey! He's got my screwdriver! Where'd you get that, you little rascal?"

Victor quickly caught the wobbly baby, who fell to his diapered bottom with a thump. He laughed and waved the tool at Victor, who quickly relieved him of it. Paul's laughter turned to tears. Mama scooped him up and took him off to bed.

Victor, now armed with his screwdriver, went back to Natalie's room. He used Mama's trick of removing the upper drawer to reach the knob-less drawer. He fished around in the front of it and quickly found the screw that had detached itself from the knob. Inserting the knob into the front of the drawer, he fit the screw in from behind it. A few quick twists of the wrist. Perfect!

"There you are, Natalie!" he declared happily. "Good as new."

"Thanks," Natalie's muffled voice came from under her blankets. "But Mama can get pajamas out even without a knob."

\*     \*     \*

Before Victor even realized it, school was out for Easter vacation, and it was Good Friday. There was no school, but Mama piled everyone into the car to head to church for Stations of the Cross. When they got to church, Mama didn't park in the closest parking place like she usually did. Instead, she parked on the other side of the parking lot. Everyone piled out of the car, and Bernadette started leading them to the church door.

"Not that way," called Mama. "Come this way."

She led them to a tall, hinged gate next to the rectory where Father lived. Mama had a little book in her hand, too, Victor noticed. They all went through the gate and found themselves in a lovely sort of garden. It was all surrounded by a tall fence, so you could not see in from outside. Victor looked around. He had not imagined that this large space was hidden away here right next to the church. He had always supposed that the gate just led to a little yard, but this was much different.

A winding, paved sidewalk meandered around the garden. It curved gently to avoid lovely trees full of delicate pink blossoms. Victor recognized a lilac bush that was starting to put on leaves and buds. The sharp, green points of daffodils and tulips stretched up toward the sun. A few already had buds swelling, nearly ready to open. Little crocuses were opened up close to the ground. Purple, white, and yellow blooms dotted the flower beds along the path.

But the unexpected part of this quiet, hidden garden was the statues. Victor and his brothers and sisters followed the cement path with their eyes. Roughly every fifteen feet along the path was a large statue. Most of them showed Jesus, and usually His cross was there, too. Many of them included another figure as well. Since they were outdoors, they were not covered in purple like the indoor statues.

"Where are we, Mama?" asked Bernadette.

"This is the Stations of the Cross garden," Mama answered. "It's such a lovely day, and I know that I'll never succeed in making Paul, Natalie, and Matthew all sit through Stations of the Cross in the church. I thought we'd pray them in the garden. Just us."

"Why have we never been here before?" questioned Victor.

"Oh, I need to have some secrets from you!" Mama answered with a smile. "Here's how we will do it: I will read the name of the Station and say the first half of the prayer. 'We adore You, oh Christ, and we praise You.' Do you remember the response?"

"Because by Your Holy Cross You have redeemed the world," Victor and Bernadette answered together.

"Very good," Mama affirmed. "Oh, and we'll kneel on the part that I say. Then after that prayer, I'll read about the Station, we say another prayer, and then we sing a verse of a song, just like when we pray them in the church. Here," she handed Victor and Bernadette each a half-size paper with the hymn printed on it. "Here are the words of the song. It's called *Stabat Mater*. That's the Latin name. Well, really just the first two words of the song in Latin. It means, 'The Mother stood,' but you need the next word of the line to get a better title. We call it 'Sorrowful Mother,' and we'll sing it in English, anyway, so we can understand what we're singing. I noticed you don't sing this one at all during the Stations when you pray them at school. It is one of my very favorite hymns, though."

It was the best Stations of the Cross ever. They were outside enjoying the sunshine and the gentle breeze. There was no sitting down. There was no droopy organ music or dim light. Paul practiced walking and falling on his bottom, and it didn't bother anyone's prayer. Mama only had to hush Natalie one time when she was giggling too much at a particularly comical tumble that Paul took. Mama's voice joined with Victor and Bernadette in that beautiful, haunting hymn about Mary's sadness. The sound of it floated through the garden and the trees and the statues, making the garden peacefully alive with their prayer.

> *At the cross her station keeping,*
> *Stood the mournful mother weeping,*
> *Close to Jesus to the last.*

When they arrived back at home, Mama asked if they'd like to dye Easter Eggs. But Victor wasn't ready to dye eggs yet. The heavy sadness of the Stations of the Cross was still with him. Somehow, during those prayers in the garden, the story of Jesus and His Cross had become real. How could a real person have nails pounded through His hands and through His feet? Right *through!* Once, Victor had

been stapling a booklet together. The stapler slipped, and he got a staple stuck in his thumb. That was just a tiny staple a little way in, but it had hurt so much! Imagine a big fat nail…all the way through.

"No thanks, Mom. I'm still thinking about those nails going all the way through Jesus' hands. That doesn't set me up for dying eggs."

"I understand," answered Mama. "Let's save the eggs up for tomorrow morning. Maybe you'd like to draw a picture of Jesus—on the cross or in the tomb?"

"Good idea."

"Yeah, good idea," Bernadette echoed. "Eggs will be better tomorrow. Good Friday is too sad for bright and funny and pretty eggs."

# Egg Dying

## CHAPTER NINE

Saturday morning—Holy Saturday morning, that is—was glorious and sunny. As soon as everyone had finished breakfast, Mama set up hard boiled eggs to dye. Since the outdoors were so gloriously sunny and not too cold, Mama spread a plastic tablecloth on the backyard picnic table and gathered all the kids and all the boiled eggs. She helped the little kids fasten their smocks at the backs of their necks. Victor and Bernadette had fastened their own already.

"OK," she began. "I boiled twenty-four eggs. Two of them broke in the pot of boiling water. We have five kids. But Paul is too little to color his own. So each kid—"

"What is this," Victor interrupted. "Math class?"

"I suppose that does sound like a math problem!" Mama laughed.

"And I know the answer!" cried Bernadette jubilantly. "Each kid, except Paul, gets to dye five eggs. Then there are two left over, so Mama can help Paul do those or just leave them white. Or, I can help Paul do one and Victor can help Paul do the other one. Or—"

"Correct!" Mama interrupted this time. "Five per little customer with two left over. Have fun!" With that, she scooped up Paul and headed into the house to start some Easter baking.

Bernadette, Victor, Matthew, and Natalie each selected an egg and moved with it toward a big red plastic cup full of coloring. One by one, they dunked their eggs and watched them settle under the colored liquid. Then they waited. Victor fished his egg out quickly. It was a pale shade of blue, a very pale shade of blue.

"Well this is boring," he declared as he let it sink down to the bottom of his cup again. "Matthew, maybe we could build an automatic egg-dying machine. It could select the white egg from the dish, drop it in the coloring, wait about five minutes, then scoop it out again! It will be awesome!"

"Let's do it!" agreed Matthew.

Both boys left their eggs in cups of dye and ran off to find some supplies to make the amazing egg dying machine.

"Hey!" called Bernadette after them. "What if I want to use green or blue on *my* egg?" She waited a moment to see if either of her brothers had heard or would answer her question. "Well, I guess I'll just take

95

your eggs out when I need to," she commented to no one in particular.

Forty-five minutes later, Victor and Matthew had successfully rigged up a solution with long-handled slotted spoon and a mechanical kitchen timer. The egg sat on the spoon in the dye, and when the dial of the timer clicked over to zero, it knocked over a toothpick on which the spoon was resting. That caused the handle of the spoon to fall and the egg to catapult out of the egg dye and the dye to drain into a shallower dish. That way, the spoon could hold the egg gently while it was dying.

The timer clicked over to zero—bing! The toothpick fell. A vividly purple egg rose quickly on its spoon, teetered, and tumbled to the table with a crack.

"Ugh!" shouted Victor.

"Argh!" groaned Matthew.

"Well," said Victor. "We're out of eggs. It works OK. I just don't know how to make it smoother or how to make it lower into the color. I guess we're finished for this year." Victor looked around. "I know! Let's go for a bike ride. It's practically like spring!"

"OK," agreed Matthew.

The brothers ran to the garage to get their bikes. Matthew frowned at his.

"Look, Victor," he pointed to the rear tire. "Totally flat!"

After finding the bike pump, Victor showed Matthew how to secure the nozzle of it to the valve of his bike tire and then pump the handle. Victor pumped. Then he let Matthew pump. He squeezed the tire with his hand. Still mushy. They each pumped a bit more.

"Quiet!" Victor said sharply and suddenly. "Hear that? It's hissing. It's a huge leak. You need a new tube," he concluded in dismay.

\*       \*       \*

"No bike ride?" Mama inquired as her two biggest boys shuffled sadly through the kitchen. She and Bernadette were rolling out pie crust, and Natalie was on the floor building block towers and letting Paul knock them over.

"No," mumbled Victor. "Matthew's bike needs a new inner tube."

"Oh, that's too bad," commented Mama, still rolling crust. "Wait a moment," she looked up from the crust. "Does Matthew still ride the littlest bike? The blue one?"

"Yes," answered Victor, looking up at Mama. "Why?"

"I think I may have a spare that will fit it. It's the same size as my double baby jogger wheels. I bought a new one for that…" She was rummaging around in a kitchen catch-all drawer. "Ah-hah!" she called, holding up a small box.

She handed the box with the inner tube to Victor.

"Think you two can change it out by yourselves? I'm pretty busy here. I'm not sure what Daddy's working on, though. He may be able to help you."

"You bet we can fix it!" cried Victor happily. "Come on, Matthew! Let's get this fixed up and go for a ride!"

After quite a bit of tugging, prying with the screwdriver, and more tugging, Victor had mostly freed the leaky tube. It was stuck on the chain. Victor groaned.

"Back tire!" he exclaimed. "Why did it have to be the back tire!"

Despite his frustration, Victor managed to take the chain off the gears with only a little bit of trouble, thanks to Matthew's help.

"Matthew, could you hand me the new tube?" Victor asked.

Matthew removed the deflated tube from the box and handed it to his brother.

"Thanks," acknowledged Victor. "Screwdriver?"

His younger brother slapped it into his hand.

"Air pump?"

It appeared next to him. Pump, pump, pump. Squeeze with the hand—nice! Some tugging and a bit of frustration to fit the chain back onto the gears. Finished!

Matthew hopped on the bike and did a loop in the driveway. "Great!" he hollered. "Thanks, Victor!"

After shouting through the front door to let Mama know, the two boys grabbed their helmets and took off down the driveway for the first bike ride of spring.

# Easter Morning

## CHAPTER TEN

"Hurry, hurry!"

Victor heard Mama's voice from the living room. He glanced at the clock. It read 10:15. "Plenty of time, Mama!" he called back to her.

She appeared in the doorway of his bedroom. She looked at him severely. "There is most certainly NOT plenty of time, Victor. *Everyone* goes to Mass on Easter Sunday. It will be packed to the doors. Now close that book and—Oh? What book is that? Wow—

is that really what a jet engine looks like? Stop distracting me! Get up and get dressed! You too, Matthew!"

She thrust a hanger with clothes at Victor and another at Matthew. "These are your new Easter clothes. Put them on quickly!" She hurried off to command the girls to get ready.

Victor surveyed his new black pants and light yellow dress shirt, complete with tie. He looked at Matthew's new clothes. Same kind of pants, but Matthew had a light blue shirt to put on. Not too bad. Victor thought his pants looked like they would stay up without a belt.

Finally, everyone had been bustled into the minivan, driven to church, and bustled out again. The ushers eyed the large family with concern and pointed them to a row right up front. Inside, the church was full of people, flowers, and hats. Victor looked around at all the hats on the women and girls as he followed his parents to their seats. Not everyone wore a hat, but he thought they looked fun. Mama and his sisters all had new hats on.

"Mama, why do only the girls wear hats?" he whispered once he was seated next to her in their pew.

"I'll have to answer that after Mass," she answered as Paul took a curious swipe at her own hat, and the bell rang to stand for the opening hymn. Mama joined the cantor, the choir, Father John, and the rest of the church as they sang loudly:

> *Alleluia, alleluia, alleluia!*
> *The strife is o'er the battle done,*
> *The crown of victory is won;*
> *The song of triumph has begun!*
> *Alleluia!*

Victor looked up at Jesus on the big crucifix in the front of the church. He joined in singing the Alleluias and thought about saying those Stations of the Cross in the garden. Was that really only two days ago? Singing alleluias, surrounded by flowers and hats on Easter Sunday morning—it still didn't make sense why Jesus chose to go on the cross like that. But when every person in church was smiling and celebrating, it almost made sense.

A family that Victor didn't know brought the bread and wine up to Father John, who returned to the altar. Shortly after, everyone knelt down and father began a prayer that Victor knew he heard at every Mass, but hadn't really noticed before. "On the day before He was to suffer, He took bread into His holy and venerable hands..."

*On the day before He was to suffer – that would be Good Friday. So the day before is Thursday. I guess father is talking about the Last Supper.*

"...and with eyes raised to heaven, to You, O God, His almighty Father, giving You thanks, He said the blessing, broke the bread and gave it to His disciples saying..."

*He gave the bread to His disciples. Father is about to give us the bread at communion. It's almost like we're sharing the Last Supper.*

"Take this all of you and eat of it: for this is my Body which will be given up for you."

*Jesus did this at the Last Supper... Maybe we should call it First Supper instead of Last Supper. Because it was the first Mass! That's what Sister Miguel Pro said last week, but it didn't make sense. But now it does. And we're like the disciples. All of us get to be like the disciples when we go up and father gives us communion. It's not really Father John handing us bread, it's really a lot more like Jesus handing us Himself.*

And Victor smiled. Somehow, it did make sense. Jesus dying on the cross – because he knew that His disciples would tell the whole world and keep blessing and breaking bread and giving it to more and more disciples for years and years and years.

Victor leaned over and tugged at the sleeve of Mama's Easter dress. "Mama!" he whispered. "Mama, Easter Mass is like the Last Supper! And we're like the disciples!"

Mama smiled, nodded, and whispered, "Every Mass, Victor. Every Mass is like that."

How about that, thought Victor. Every single Mass. Sometimes Mass seemed long. But he hadn't thought about being at Mass as a disciple before. Victor looked around the church and saw the flowers and the hats and the statues. Those decorations made Mass beautiful. But being there, at the Last Supper, being a disciple, begin asked by Jesus Himself to "Do this in memory of me." That made Mass amazing. Victor made a promise in his heart that he would try to do Mass in memory of Jesus every time. He'd try not to complain about Mass. And he knew he'd be able to do it (sometimes, anyway) because, after all, the disciples had, even with emperors and stuff telling them not to and putting them in jail.

\*       \*       \*

Matthew and Natalie burst into the living room after Mass. "Where are the Easter baskets?" Natalie demanded putting her hands on her little hips.

"Well, I need to set them up still," replied Mama. She passed Paul off to Daddy and hurried away, presumably in search of the baskets.

"What do we do now?" asked Daddy as he looked around the room.

Victor and Bernadette looked at him. They knew by the tone of his voice that he must have a good idea.

"What? What is it?" demanded Bernadette. "You have an idea! I can tell!"

Daddy winked at her. "Where are those eggs you dyed? Let's go outside and hide them for Mama. Then she'll have to find all the eggs this year!"

"But what about us?" Bernadette asked, looking concerned.

"Don't worry," Daddy answered. "Mama and I will just hide them again for you!"

"Great!" shouted Victor. "I'll get the eggs."

Not long after all the eggs that had survived the dying process had been secreted away, Mama popped out the back door.

"You may come in for Easter baskets!" she announced triumphantly. She looked around at Bernadette, Victor, Natalie, Matthew, Paul, and Daddy. "What's going on?" she queried them all. "Even Paul looks like he's up to something!"

"We made a hunt for you!" cried Natalie. "It's your turn to hunt the eggs!"

Mama laughed and smiled a kiss at Daddy. "Baskets first!" she insisted. "Then I'll play your little game."

The kids jostled past each other through the back door and into the living room. Bernadette ran to the pink and green basket she'd had since she was two. She oohed and aahed over a jar of bubble solution, new tights, and a jump rope. Natalie ran to her purple basket and squealed with delight at a miniature baby doll only three inches high, her own bottle of bubbles, and little socks with lace around the top edge. Mama led Paul to a basket, unwrapped a chocolate bunny from it and handed it to the happy baby. Matthew trotted over to the last remaining basket and pulled out

his treats. Victor looked around. He did not see the basket he saw every year. He looked curiously at Daddy, who was standing with a big smile on his face. There, at Daddy's feet sat a shiny red tool box. Victor looked up at Daddy. Daddy nodded. Victor ran to the box. He didn't have an Easter basket—he had an Easter tool box! He opened it up.

Needle-nose pliers, like he had used to fix the Rosary.

A handsome set of Allen wrenches, like he had used to fix the chair.

A bottle of wood glue, also from fixing the chair.

Pliers and a crescent wrench, like he had used to fix the toilet at school.

Phillips screwdriver, the one he and Daddy had picked out together. He could put his flathead screwdriver in, too. Under all the tools lay a small stack of papers. Victor picked them up and looked at them curiously. After a minute, he realized they were plans. Possibly for a small house? He kept reading them, no longer paying attention to his sisters and brothers blowing bubbles and laughing. Victor kept studying his new plans. They included measurements and instructions. They seemed to be for a very small house.

Finally, Daddy chuckled. "Did you figure it out yet, Victor?"

Victor looked up. "It looks like a little house. I don't quite understand it."

"It's a tree house!" Daddy grinned. "And you have all the tools it requires. I have already cut the lumber to size, so there is no sawing required. Let's go!"

# Lent, Rosary,
# Stations of the Cross

---

## PARENT'S GUIDE

In the story, I wanted to show a Catholic family living their faith together. I hope that some of the events in Victor's fictional family can spark conversation and opportunities for teaching and learning with the families of my readers. In case parents would like more information about some of the religious observances and devotions in the book, I'm including a parent's guide. It's a general introduction to the Catholic observance of Lent, the devotional prayer of the Rosary, and the Stations of Cross. You don't need to read it, but if you have questions about these practices or how you could introduce them in your family, read on.

113

# LENT

I love the gift of the liturgical year. The
Catholic Church, in its long history has seen that faith
is never static. When faith becomes still, it dies. So,
through the changing of the seasons, different parts of
our faith are emphasized and renewed. The season of
Lent begins with Ash Wednesday and extends until
Easter. We say that it is forty days, but that is only if
you do not tally the Sundays of Lent as you count the
days. On Sundays, we always celebrate the
resurrection, so those days are not days of Lent. It is a
season of penance – we emphasize prayer and fasting
as we look forward to Jesus' passion and death on
Good Friday. We pray and fast with Jesus, as He
prayed before beginning His ministry: "Then Jesus
was led by the Spirit into the wilderness to be tempted
by the devil. After fasting forty days and forty nights,
He was hungry." (Matthew 4: 1-2) But it is interesting
to note that the number forty is quite common in the
history of our faith and that the forty days of Lent can

bring to mind many occurrences: Noah and his family were in the ark while it rained for forty days and nights. Moses was on the mountain for forty days talking with God. Moses led the people of Israel through the desert for forty years before they reached the promised land. Jesus spent forty days on earth after His resurrection before ascending to heaven.

As a family, it's a great time to renew family prayer traditions. Or begin them! Take a look at your spiritual life as a family and ask how it can improve: Should we add a prayer before dinner? Should we make an effort to all *be* at dinner together? Should we add prayers at bedtime? Should we turn off the TV and read or play games together? Should we renew our commitment to Sunday Mass? Should we renew our commitment to get to Sunday Mass on time? Should we try to get to Mass an additional day during the week?

If you're looking for more suggestions as to how to observe Lent, you can check out catholic.com or osv.com and do a search. *The Little Oratory* by Leila Lawler and David Clayton has a nice chapter on Lent.

Author Leila Lawler also has a blog (LikeMotherLikeDaughter.org) with lots of liturgical year suggestions.

## ROSARY

The Rosary is one of those defining symbols that is uniquely Catholic. But if you didn't grow up with it or it was never well-explained, it can be hard to understand this prayer. The title "Rosary" is possibly more than a thousand years old and developed into our modern Rosary from other repeated prayers kept track of by strings of beads. St. Dominic greatly popularized praying the Rosary (in a slightly different form than we pray today) beginning in 1214.

Our Lady of Lourdes prayed the Rosary with St. Bernadette in 1858. In 1917, Our Lady appeared at Fatima and encouraged the children there to pray the Rosary and ask others to do so as well. Pope Saint John XXIII encouraged the faithful to pray the rosary with, "mystical contemplation, intimate reflection, and pious intention." (ca 1960) and wrote that, "the Rosary of Mary, considered in its various elements, which are linked together in vocal prayer and woven into it as in a delicate and rich embroidery, full of spiritual warmth and beauty." Pope Saint John Paul the Great added five new mysteries (the Luminous) to the Rosary in 2002, which he declared "the Year of the Rosary." And, if you live in Wyandotte, Michigan, you can walk a three mile loop and pass twenty front yard Rosary shrines – one for each mystery. (A project initiated by my mother!)

As a prayer, it offers a chance to meditate on twenty specific moments (called mysteries) in the life of Christ. As we meditate on each mystery, we pray one Our Father followed by ten Hail Marys (a decade). The Rosary is divided into four sets of mysteries. A complete Rosary includes five decades.

Mysteries of the Rosary:

Joyful Mysteries

1. The Annunciation
2. The Visitation
3. The Nativity

4. The Presentation

5. The Finding in the Temple

Luminous Mysteries

1. Baptism of Jesus in the Jordan

2. The Miracle at the Wedding at Cana

3. The Proclamation of the Kingdom

4. The Transfiguration

5. The Institution of the Eucharist

The Sorrowful Mysteries

1. The Agony in the Garden

2. The Scourging at the Pillar

3. The Crowning with Thorns

4. The Carrying of the Cross

5. The Crucifixion and Death of Our Lord Jesus Christ

The Glorious Mysteries

1. The Resurrection

2. The Ascension

3. The Descent of the Holy Spirit

4. The Assumption of Mary into Heaven

5.  The Crowning of Mary, Queen of Heaven and Earth

There are many wonderful books and meditations on the Rosary. The United States Conference of Catholic Bishops (USCCB) has good instructions on their website: www.usccb.org (then search "how to pray the Rosary"). Most Catholic bookstores and Catholic church gift shops have little pamphlets of a similar title. *The Holy Rosary* by Fr. Lovasik is written for children and has a very nice explanation of each mystery. It's widely available. *Scriptural Rosary for Children* by Rev. Jude Winkler and *Child's Guide to the Rosary* by Elizabeth Ficocelli are also very nice for children.

A great addition to a family Rosary is pictures of the mysteries for children to look at. There's a great Rosary "flip book" with 16th century artwork depicting each mystery. (Disclosure: my brother put it together!) It's available through Amazon; search "Rosary Flip Book."

# STATIONS OF THE CROSS

I love to pray Stations of the Cross with my children on Fridays of Lent. It's a Friday afternoon tradition that they expect. I have pictures of each station (mine are from Catholic Heritage Curricula: www.chcweb.com) that we look at, and we pray a short prayer with each one. Unlike the rosary, there's not as much of a defined "right way" to pray Stations of the Cross. There are fourteen stations; distinct moments on Jesus' walk to His death.

1. Jesus is condemned to death.
2. Jesus accepts His Cross.
3. Jesus falls for the first time.
4. Jesus meets His sorrowful Mother.
5. Simon of Cyrene helps Jesus carry the Cross.
6. Veronica wipes the face of Jesus.
7. Jesus falls for the second time.
8. Jesus meets the women of Jerusalem.

9. Jesus falls for the third time.

10. Jesus is stripped of His garments.

11. Jesus is nailed to His Cross.

12. Jesus dies on the Cross. (all kneel in silence for a moment.)

13. Jesus is taken down from the Cross.

14. Jesus is laid in the Tomb.

There's a short prayer that is usually recited at the beginning of each station:

**Leader**: We adore You, O Christ, and we bless You.

**Response**: Because by Your Holy Cross You have redeemed the world.

Then, depending on how many and how small the children you're praying with are, you can pray a short prayer, several prayers, read a meditation aloud, and / or sing a verse of a song. Good song choices are the *Stabat Mater* (At the Cross Her Station Keeping), Were You There?, or Jesus, Remember Me.

Sometimes I take my kids on a walk around our block as we pray. On Good Friday, I like to go to a church or statue garden and walk around as we pray. Sometimes we just sit on the couch and look at the pictures as we pray the stations. But walking during this prayer can be a very powerful way to join in Jesus' suffering as He walked up Calvary under the weight of His Cross and our sins.

The USCCB website has several different ways to pray the stations, which include excerpts from the Bible. It's always great to use Scripture itself with our children, and there.  Some other good book(lets) for children that do this are *The Stations of the Cross for Children: a Dramatized Presentation* by Rita Coleman, *Walking with Jesus to Calvary: Stations of the Cross for Children* by Angela M. Burrin, and *The Way of the Cross for Children* by Rev. Jude Winkler, OFM.

# About the Author

Emily Ortega earned a Bachelor of Science in chemistry from Case Western Reserve University. After working for two years as a campus missionary with FOCUS, the Fellowship of Catholic University Students, Emily earned her Master's degree in Humanities from Stanford University. She currently resides with her husband and their seven children in Sedona, Arizona. She's excited to bring a fictional Catholic family to life and offer young Catholic readers the possibility that their lives in a big, Catholic family aren't really that odd.

# About the Illustrator

 Meg Whalen studied business at Elon University in North Carolina, but soon after realized that her talents and passions were pulling her in a different direction. Inspired from a young age by comic strips like Calvin & Hobbes and gaining a new appreciation for the beauty in children's books, she moved to Denver and audited the children's book illustration program at Rocky Mountain College of Art & Design. While living in Denver, she also completed a master's degree in Theology at the Augustine Institute. She now lives in Florida with her husband, Danny, and their daughter, Rosie.